It's Great to Be EIGHT

This book belongs to:

Miss Lindsay Burke

A
LITTLE APPLE
PAPERBACK

SCHOLASTIC INC.
New York Toronto London Auckland Sydney
Mexico City New Delhi Hong Kong

Contents

Introduction

"Everybody old had once been young. That was a fact. Everyone in the world — even people older than Grandfather — had started out as a baby. Of course Thomas knew this, but it was one of those things he knew, and could not make himself *believe*." This is how Thomas, the main character of Mary Stolz's book *Go Fish*, feels, and probably how you feel sometimes. Believe it or not, even your parents were once eight years old! And so were all of the authors of these stories. There are certain things that almost everyone experiences, such as the first day of school, fighting with your best friend, getting the measles, and even losing someone you love.

In this book you'll meet twelve incredible characters, such as Charlie Bucket, the hero of *Charlie and the Chocolate Factory*, by the World's Most Scrumdiddlyumptious Storyteller, Roald Dahl. Charlie is just a regular, honest kid who experiences something he will never forget when he meets the amazing Willy

Wonka; and the very messy, but very lovable Amber from *Amber Brown Is Not a Crayon* by Paula Danziger. Amber's got just one problem — she's about to lose her best friend. You'll meet kids that can't seem to stay out of trouble, such as Katie from Patricia Hermes' *Christmas Magic* and Ramona from Beverly Cleary's book. And many more courageous characters from authors such as the very funny Louis Sachar and Newbery Medal–winner Patricia MacLachlan.

Also included are two original, never-before-published stories by the best-selling author of The Baby-sitters Club series, Ann M. Martin, and by Newbery Honor and Coretta Scott King Award–winning writer Patricia McKissack.

These stories will remind you that being eight can be magical and wonderful, sometimes lonely and hard, but always an incredible adventure. Collected here are twelve great authors known for their humor and warmth. Twelve great stories to remind you: It's great to be eight!

From
Ramona Quimby, Age 8
by Beverly Cleary

8

Almost every kid knows Ramona the Pest, who is now eight and about to begin the first day of third grade. Ramona thinks this is the best day ever, until she gets on the bus and meets Danny. He kicks her seat and steals her new pink eraser, and school hasn't even started yet!

Beverly Cleary's funny book about Ramona won a Newbery Honor.

The bus stopped at Cedarhurst, Ramona's new school, a two-story red-brick building very much like her old school. As the children hopped out of the bus, Ramona felt a little thrill of triumph. She had not been carsick. She now discovered she felt as if she had grown even more than her feet. Third-graders were the biggest people — except teachers, of course — at this school. All the little first- and second-graders running around the playground, looking so young, made Ramona feel tall, grown-up, and sort of . . . well, wise in the ways of the world.

Danny shoved ahead of her. "Catch!" he yelled to another boy. Something small and pink flew through the air and into the second boy's cupped hands. The boy wound up as if he were pitching a base-ball, and the eraser flew back to Danny.

"You gimme back my eraser!" Encumbered by her lunch box, Ramona chased Danny, who ran, ducking and dodging, among the first- and second-graders. When she was about to catch him, he tossed her eraser to the other boy. If her lunch box had not banged against her knees, Ramona might have been able to grab him. Unfortunately, the bell rang first.

"Yard apes!" yelled Ramona, her name for the sort of boys who always got the best balls, who were always first on the playground, and who chased their soccer balls through other people's hopscotch games. She saw her pink eraser fly back into Danny's hands. "Yard apes!" she yelled again, tears of anger in her eyes. "Yucky yard apes!" The boys, of course, paid no attention.

Still fuming, Ramona entered her new school and climbed the stairs to find her assigned classroom, which she discovered looked out over roofs and treetops to Mount Hood in the distance. I wish it would erupt, she thought, because she felt like exploding with anger.

Ramona's new room was filled with excitement and confusion. She saw some people she had known at her old school. Others were strangers. Everyone was talking at once, shouting greetings to old friends or looking over those who would soon become new friends, rivals, or enemies. Ramona missed Howie, who had been assigned to another room, but wouldn't you know? That yard ape, Danny, was sitting at a desk, still wearing his baseball cap and tossing Ramona's new eraser from one hand to another. Ramona was too frustrated to speak. She wanted to hit him. How dare he spoil her day?

"All right, you guys, quiet down," said the teacher.

5

Ramona was startled to hear her class called "you guys." Most teachers she had known would say something like, "I feel I am talking very loud. Is it because the room is noisy?" She chose a chair at a table at the front of the room and studied her new teacher, a strong-looking woman with short hair and a deep tan. Like my swimming teacher, thought Ramona.

"My name is Mrs. Whaley," said the teacher, as she printed her name on the blackboard. "*W-h-a-l-e-y*. I'm a whale with a *y* for a tail." She laughed and so did her class. Then the whale with a *y* for a tail handed Ramona some slips of paper. "Please pass these out," she directed. "We need some name tags until I get to know you."

Ramona did as she was told, and as she walked among the desks she discovered her new sandals squeaked. *Squeak, creak, squeak*. Ramona giggled, and so did the rest of the class. *Squeak, creak, squeak*. Ramona went up one aisle and down the other. The last person she gave a slip to was the boy from the bus, who was still wearing his baseball cap. "You give me back my eraser, you yard ape!" she whispered.

"Try and get it, Bigfoot," he whispered back with a grin.

Ramona stared at her feet. Bigfoot? Bigfoot was a hairy creature ten feet tall, who was supposed to leave huge footprints in the mountain snows of southern Oregon. Some people thought they had seen Bigfoot slipping through the forests, but no one had ever been able to prove he really existed.

Bigfoot indeed! Ramona's feet had grown, but they were not huge. She was not going to let him get away with this insult. "Superfoot to you, Yard Ape," she said right out loud, realizing too late that she had given herself a new nickname.

To her astonishment, Yard Ape pulled her eraser out of his pocket and handed it to her with a grin. Well! With her nose in the air, Ramona squeaked back to her seat. She felt so triumphant that she returned the longest way around and bent her feet as much as she could to make the loudest possible squeaks. She had done the right thing! She had not let Yard Ape upset her by calling her Bigfoot, and now she had her eraser in her hand. He would probably call her Superfoot forever, but she did not care. Superfoot was a name she had given herself. That made all the difference. She had won.

Ramona became aware that she was squeaking in the midst of an unusual silence. She stopped midsqueak when she saw her new teacher watching her with a little smile. The class was watching the teacher.

"We all know you have musical shoes," said Mrs. Whaley. Of course the class laughed.

By walking with stiff legs and not bending her feet, Ramona reached her seat without squeaking at all. She did not know what to think. At first she thought Mrs. Whaley's remark was a reprimand, but then maybe her teacher was just trying to be funny. She couldn't tell about grown-ups sometimes. Ramona finally decided that any teacher who would let Yard Ape wear his baseball cap in the classroom wasn't really fussy about squeaking shoes.

Ramona bent over her paper and wrote slowly and carefully in cursive, Ramona Quimby, age 8. She admired the look of what she had written, and she was happy. She liked feeling tall in her new school. She liked — or was pretty sure she liked — her nonfussy teacher. Yard Ape — Well, he was a problem, but so far she had not let him get the best of her for keeps. Besides, although she might never admit it to anyone, now that she had her eraser back she liked him — sort of. Maybe she enjoyed a challenge.

Ramona began to draw a fancy border, all scallops and curliques, around her name. She was happy, too, because her family had been happy that morning and because she was big enough for her family to depend on.

From
Charlie and the Chocolate Factory
by Roald Dahl

8

Charlie Bucket is just a regular kid who lives with his parents and grandparents on the edge of town. Like most kids, Charlie loves chocolate. This year, five children will find a golden ticket inside a Wonka candy bar. Charlie may just have the most amazing birthday ever.

Charlie entered the store and laid the damp dollar bill on the counter.

"One Wonka's Whipple-Scrumptious Fudgemallow Delight," he said, remembering how much he had loved the one he had on his birthday.

The man behind the counter looked fat and well-fed. He had big lips and fat cheeks and a very fat neck. The fat around his neck bulged out all around the top of his collar like a rubber ring. He turned and reached behind him for the candy bar, then he turned back again and handed it to Charlie. Charlie grabbed it and quickly tore off the wrapper and took an enormous bite. Then he took another . . . and another . . . and oh, the joy of being able to cram large pieces of something sweet and solid into one's mouth! The sheer blissful joy of being able to fill one's mouth with rich solid food!

"You look like you wanted that one, sonny," the shopkeeper said pleasantly.

Charlie nodded, his mouth bulging with chocolate.

The shopkeeper put Charlie's change on the counter. "Take it easy," he said. "It'll give you a gut-ache if you swallow it like that without chewing."

Charlie went on wolfing the candy. He couldn't stop. And in less than half a minute, the whole thing had disappeared down his throat. He was quite out of breath, but he felt marvelously, extraordinarily happy. He reached out a hand to take the change. Then he paused. His eyes were just above the level of the counter. They were staring at the little silver coins lying there. The coins were all dimes. There were nine of them altogether. Surely it wouldn't matter if he spent just one more. . . .

"I think," he said quietly, "I think . . . I'll have just one more of those candy bars. The same kind as before, please."

"Why not?" the fat shopkeeper said, reaching behind him again and taking another Whipple-Scrumptious Fudgemallow Delight from the shelf. He laid it on the counter.

Charlie picked it up and tore off the wrapper . . . and *suddenly* . . . from underneath the wrapper . . . there came a brilliant flash of gold.

Charlie's heart stood still.

"It's a Golden Ticket!" screamed the shopkeeper, leaping about a foot in the air. "You've got a Golden Ticket! You've found the last Golden Ticket! Hey, what do you know! Come and look at this, everybody! The kid's found Wonka's last Golden Ticket! There it is! It's right there in his hands!"

It seemed as though the shopkeeper might be going to have a fit. "In my shop, too!" he yelled. "He found it right here in my own little shop! Somebody call the newspapers quick and let them know! Watch out now, sonny! Don't tear it as you unwrap it! That thing's precious!"

In a few seconds, there was a crowd of about twenty people clustering around Charlie, and many more were pushing their way in from the street. Everybody wanted to get a look at the Golden Ticket and at the lucky finder.

"Where is it?" somebody shouted. "Hold it up so all of us can see it!"

"There it is, there!" someone else shouted. "He's holding it in his hands! See the gold shining!"

"How did *he* manage to find it, I'd like to know?" a large boy shouted angrily. "*Twenty* bars a day I've been buying for weeks and weeks!"

"Think of all the free stuff he'll be getting too!" another boy said enviously. "A lifetime supply!"

"He'll need it, the skinny little shrimp!" a girl said, laughing.

Charlie hadn't moved. He hadn't even unwrapped the Golden Ticket from around the candy bar. He was standing very still, holding it tightly with both hands while the crowd pushed and shouted all around him. He felt quite dizzy. There was a peculiar floating sensation coming over him, as though he were floating up in the air like a balloon. His feet didn't seem to be touching the ground at all. He could hear his heart thumping away loudly somewhere in his throat.

At that point, he became aware of a hand resting lightly on his shoulder, and when he looked up, he saw a tall man standing over him. "Listen," the man whispered. "I'll buy it from you. I'll give you fifty dollars. How about it, eh? And I'll give you a new bicycle as well. Okay?"

"Are you *crazy*?" shouted a woman who was standing equally close. "Why, I'd give him *five hundred* dollars for that ticket! You want to sell that ticket for five hundred dollars, young man?"

"That's *quite* enough of that!" the fat shopkeeper shouted, pushing his way through the crowd and taking Charlie firmly by the arm. "Leave the kid alone, will you! Make way there! Let him out!"

And to Charlie, as he led him to the door, he whispered, "Don't you let *anybody* have it! Take it straight home, quickly, before you lose it! Run all the way and don't stop till you get there, you understand?"

Charlie nodded.

"You know something," the fat shop-keeper said, pausing a moment and smiling at Charlie, "I have a feeling you needed a break like this. I'm awfully glad you got it. Good luck to you, sonny."

"Thank you," Charlie said, and off he went, running through the snow as fast as his legs would go. And as he flew past Mr. Willy Wonka's factory, he turned and waved at it and sang out, "I'll be seeing you! I'll be seeing you soon!" And five minutes later he arrived at his own home.

Charlie burst through the front door, shouting, "*Mother*! *Mother*! *Mother*!"

Mrs. Bucket was in the old grandparents' room, serving them their evening soup.

"*Mother*!" yelled Charlie, rushing in on them like a hurricane. "Look! I've got it! Look, Mother, look! The last Golden Ticket! It's mine! I found some money in the street and I bought two candy bars and the second one had the Golden Ticket and there were *crowds* of people all around me wanting to see it and the shopkeeper rescued me and I ran all the way home and here I am! *IT'S THE FIFTH GOLDEN TICKET, MOTHER, AND I'VE FOUND IT!"*

Mrs. Bucket simply stood and stared, while the four old grandparents, who were sitting up in bed balancing bowls of soup on their laps, all dropped their spoons with a clatter and froze against their pillows.

For about ten seconds there was absolute silence in the room. Nobody dared to speak or move. It was a magic moment.

From
Amber Brown Is Not a Crayon
by Paula Danziger

8

Amber Brown and Justin Daniels have been best friends since preschool. Not just best friends, but perfect friends. They've always helped each other out. Amber is messy and Justin is neat. So what do you do if you find out your best friend is moving away? If you're Amber Brown, you do everything to get him to stay.

"Snack time." Justin puts the package of Oreos on his kitchen table.

"Yum." I rip the package open, take out a cookie, eat the cream center out of the middle and hand the cookie parts to Justin.

"Yum." He eats them.

I take a second cookie and eat the center out of it.

Justin and I have been eating cookies like this since preschool.

We call it teamwork.

Hannah Burton calls it "gross."

Mrs. Daniels walks into the kitchen.

Danny follows. "Play Legos with me."

"Leg. Legos. What's the difference?" Justin walks over to his brother and pulls at his leg.

I wish I had a little brother or sister to tease. Being an only child means I don't, but it's okay, I guess, because I can always tease Danny.

Mrs. Daniels tells Danny, "You can play with your toys later. Right now I don't want you to make a mess because the real estate broker is bringing people over to look at the house."

Suddenly, teasing Danny doesn't seem so important. Suddenly, it's much more important to cross my fingers and wish very hard — very, very hard. I wish that the people hate the house, that they think it's too big or too small, that they don't have the money to buy it.

The doorbell rings.

"Would you two play with Danny?" Mrs. Daniels asks and then leaves to answer the door.

"Cookie." Danny imitates the sound of the Cookie Monster on *Sesame Street*.

"Sure, Walter." I hand him a cookie.

Walter is Danny's real name but when he was little he had trouble saying it and kept calling himself "Danny Danny."

The name stuck and now everyone calls him Danny, except for Justin and me when we want to torment him.

Danny starts to sing a song. "Amber Brown is a crayon . . . a crayon . . . a crayon . . . a broken old crayon."

Something tells me that I never should have let him know how I hate the way that some kids tease me about my name.

I guess that it's probably not such a good idea to tease someone about a name when they can tease back.

We all eat a few more cookies and then take a plastic bowl and start throwing cookies into it.

"Two points. Yes!" I yell, as my cookie rims the bowl and falls in.

"Good shot," a strange voice says.

Looking up, I see a very pregnant lady who applauds my athletic ability.

"Maybe Amber should try out for the gold medal in the cookie Olympics." Justin grins.

"Maybe you kids should play in another room while Mrs. Bradley looks at the kitchen." Mrs. Daniels smiles and motions us out.

"It's all right. I like seeing children in the kitchen. I've already got a four-year-old." Mrs. Bradley pats her stomach. "And this one will be here in a few months. So I like the idea of a kitchen with children playing in it." She looks around.

I debate telling her that there are dragons in the basement, ghosts in the walls, and ectoplasm in the attic.

"You've done a really nice job decorating." Mrs. Bradley is looking in a cupboard, which has shelves that twirl around.

"Thank you," Mrs. Daniels says. "We've really loved living here and hope that the next family loves it, too."

I don't want there to be a "next family" here.

I remember how we all sat around looking at wallpaper and stuff when the kitchen was being redone.

Mrs. Daniels said that since everyone in the house was going to see it every day, everyone could help decorate it. She also said that since I was practically a member of the family, I could help, too.

They didn't pick the wallpaper that Justin and I wanted, baseball players.

Instead, there are flowers all over the wall.

Mrs. Bradley says, "If you don't mind, I would like my husband to see this house soon."

Soon. That sounds serious.

I can't help myself. "I hope you don't mind alligators in the toilet."

Mrs. Bradley looks surprised and then she grins. "Alligators in the toilet. That's quite a bonus."

She and Mrs. Daniels look at each other and smile.

This is definitely not a good sign.

The grown-ups leave the room.

Justin, Danny and I continue playing cookie basketball.

We pretend that everything's the same.

I try not to get too nervous. After all, a zillion people have seen the house and not bought it.

Maybe Mrs. Bradley's husband will hate it. I hope I'm here when he looks at the house. I'll be sure to mention giant termites.

Mrs. Daniels returns.

"Amber, would you like to stay for dinner tonight? I'll call your mother and see if she wants to join us. We'll order pizza."

"Yes," I say, feeling a little better.

This is something we do a lot, especially since my parents got a divorce.

I stay with the Danielses until my mom gets home from work and then sometimes we all eat together. Pizza is Justin's and my favorite food group.

Mrs. Daniels gets on the phone.

My mother says yes.

Then Mrs. Daniels calls the pizza place. "Extra cheese, mushrooms, and sausage, please."

Justin and I yell at the same time, "And hold the anchovies."

Then we laugh, imagining what the guy looks like holding the anchovies.

And for a while, I forget that the house might get sold.

From
Christmas Magic
by Patricia Hermes

8

Katie isn't afraid of anything, except maybe Christmas. She tries so hard to be good, because if she isn't then Santa won't come. But sometimes things don't work out the way you plan. Every time Katie makes a mistake, she remembers that Santa is watching.

On Monday, Katie felt happy as she and Obie walked to the bus stop. She knew she had been good in the city yesterday. Very, very good. Maybe Santa had noticed. She'd seen him on the street corner ringing a little bell.

"Obie?" Katie said to him. She swung her backpack around in front of her. "You know about Santa?"

"What about him?" Obie said.

"Well. You're supposed to be good," she said. "Right?"

"I am good," Obie said.

"I know," Katie said. "But does he come to everybody, you think?"

"Yeah," Obie said.

"Bad people, too?" Katie said.

"Really bad?" Obie said.

"Well, maybe sort of bad," Katie said.

"Oh," Obie said. He was quiet a minute. Then he said, "I don't think so. Not to everybody."

Katie frowned. "That's what I think," she said. "And he should. He really, really should. I'm going to write and tell him."

"Don't say anything mean," Obie said.

"I won't!" Katie said.

When they got to school, Katie was still thinking.

A letter. A Santa letter. She wondered if he would answer if she wrote to him. She wondered if he would listen to what she said, that maybe some people couldn't help being bad.

She put away her coat, then went over and looked in on the rabbits in their cage. The class gerbils had run away, and now they had two pet rabbits. The class had named them Ken and Barbie. Katie wondered if the rabbits had been caught in a rabbit trap or something.

Katie turned so that her back was to the room and no one could see. Then she slid the bar out of the little metal ring and quietly opened the cage. She knew she was supposed to ask permission first, but Mrs. Henry, their teacher, was busy counting lunch slips. Besides, Katie knew she'd be careful.

Very carefully, she lifted Ken out. He was all white and fluffy and soft. She held him up against her face. She could feel his little heart beating fast against her hand. It felt like a little motor or something.

He nibbled at her neck. It tickled.

"Hey, Ken," Katie said. "Do you like it here?"

He made little snuffly sounds.

"All right, boys and girls," Mrs. Henry said then. "I want you all to get to your seats, sit up straight and tall, and listen."

Quickly, Katie slid Ken back into his cage. "'Bye, Ken," she said to him.

She closed the cage door and slid the bar across it. The bar was supposed to slide into a little metal ring. But the bar stuck. It wouldn't go all the way in the ring. She wiggled it a little. It was still stuck.

"We're waiting, Katie," Mrs. Henry said.

Katie wiggled the bar once more.

The bar still wasn't all the way inside the ring, but almost. It looked tight enough.

Katie hurried to her seat. She sat up on her knees, though, so she could still see Ken and Barbie.

Everybody in class was sitting up straight and tall. Emil Marks stuck his shoulders back like he was in the army.

Katie had never seen Emil do that before. Actually, she had never seen him sit still before.

She wondered how long he could stay like that.

"Everybody ready?" Mrs. Henry said. She was looking at Katie.

Katie unfolded her legs. She sat up straight and tall.

Next to Katie on one side, her friend Amelia sat up straight, too.

On the other side of Katie, Tiffany sat up straight. Her hands were folded on her desk, and her hair was brushed straight back into a ponytail. Even the pencils on her desk were straight. Her back was the straightest of all. Everything about Tiffany was perfect. Except that she was the meanest girl in the class. Perfectly mean.

Katie tried to sit as straight as Tiffany.

It made her back hurt.

"Ouch!" she said.

"Katie, are you listening?" Mrs. Henry said.

Katie felt her ears get hot.

She nodded.

"All right then, boys and girls," Mrs. Henry said. "This is what we are going to do today."

She held up a little box. In it were folded scraps of paper.

"These are your names in here," Mrs. Henry said. "Each person's name is on a slip of paper. I'm going to go up and down the aisle and each of you is to take out a piece of paper — a name. Just take it, but don't look at it yet."

31

"Why not?" Emil called out. He didn't raise his hand.

Mrs. Henry looked at Emil. She did her wide-eyed look.

Emil raised his hand.

He was always forgetting to do that.

"Yes, Emil?" Mrs. Henry said in her I-want-to-be-friends voice.

"Why can't we look?" Emil said.

"You'll see in a minute," Mrs. Henry said. "This is about being a Secret Santa. And you know what a Secret Santa does?"

"What?" Emil said.

Mrs. Henry smiled. "Each day next week, you bring in a present for the person whose name you get," she said. "And each day you'll get a present because somebody has your name. But it's a secret. You can't tell whose name you have. You'll be a Secret Santa."

"There is no Santa," Tiffany muttered.

Mrs. Henry didn't hear, but Katie did.

Katie made a witch face at Tiffany.

Tiffany pretended not to see.

"I'll tell you more in a minute," Mrs.

Henry said. "Just sit still until we each have a name."

She started up and down the aisles.

Amelia, Katie's best friend, smiled at Katie.

"I love secrets!" Amelia whispered.

"Me, too!" Katie whispered back.

Each person picked a name.

When it was Katie's turn, she shuffled all the little slips around.

She smiled up at Mrs. Henry.

Mrs. Henry smiled back.

Katie picked a little folded piece of paper. She held it in her hand while Mrs. Henry went down the aisle. She wondered whose name she had picked.

And then she had a really bad thought. What if she had picked Tiffany? What if she had to be a Secret Santa to perfectly mean Tiffany?

Very carefully, Katie unfolded one end of her paper.

She looked all around her.

No one was looking.

Katie slid the paper under her desk. She laid it on her knee. She unfolded it until it was flat.

She bent to peek at it.

"Mrs. Henry!" Tiffany called out. "Katie's peeking."

"I am not!" Katie said. She crumpled up the paper. She could feel her ears get hot.

"That's enough, Katie and Tiffany," Mrs. Henry said. She didn't turn to look at them.

Katie turned to Tiffany. She made her best witch face.

"Santa saw that!" Tiffany whispered.

"So?" Katie whispered back. "You said there is no Santa."

Tiffany shrugged. She smiled, a mean smile.

"Maybe there isn't," she said. "But maybe there is."

From
Sarah, Plain and Tall
by Patricia MacLachlan

8

Anna and Caleb dream of the day when Sarah will come. They have been lonely since their mother died. Maybe Sarah will marry Papa and be their new mother. But Sarah comes from near the sea. Will she be able to leave it behind and call the prairie home?

Patricia MacLachlan's moving story of a family looking for someone to love them won the Newbery Medal in 1985.

Sarah came in the spring. She came through green grass fields that bloomed with Indian paintbrush, red and orange, and blue-eyed grass.

Papa got up early for the long day's trip to the train and back. He brushed his hair so slick and shiny that Caleb laughed. He wore a clean blue shirt, and a belt instead of suspenders.

He fed and watered the horses, talking to them as he hitched them up to the wagon. Old Bess, calm and kind; Jack, wild-eyed, reaching over to nip Bess on the neck.

"Clear day, Bess," said Papa, rubbing her nose.

"Settle down, Jack." He leaned his head on Jack.

And then Papa drove off along the dirt road to fetch Sarah. Papa's new wife. Maybe. Maybe our new mother.

Gophers ran back and forth across the road, stopping to stand up and watch the wagon. Far off in the field a woodchuck ate and listened. Ate and listened.

Caleb and I did our chores without talking. We shoveled out the stalls and laid down new hay. We fed the sheep. We swept and straightened and carried wood and water. And then our chores were done.

Caleb pulled on my shirt.

"Is my face clean?" he asked. "Can my face be *too* clean?" He looked alarmed.

"No, your face is clean but not too clean," I said.

Caleb slipped his hand into mine as we stood on the porch, watching the road. He was afraid.

"Will she be nice?" he asked. "Like Maggie?"

"Sarah will be nice," I told him.

"How far away is Maine?" he asked.

"You know how far. Far away, by the sea."

"Will Sarah bring some sea?" he asked.

"No, you cannot bring the sea."

The sheep ran in the field, and far off the cows moved slowly to the pond, like turtles.

"Will she like us?" asked Caleb very softly.

I watched a marsh hawk wheel down behind the barn.

He looked up at me.

"Of course she will like us." He answered his own question. "We are nice," he added, making me smile.

We waited and watched. I rocked on the porch and Caleb rolled a marble on the wood floor. Back and forth. Back and forth. The marble was blue.

We saw the dust from the wagon first,

rising above the road, above the heads of Jack and Old Bess. Caleb climbed up onto the porch roof and shaded his eyes.

"A bonnet!" he cried. "I see a yellow bonnet!"

The dogs came out from under the porch, ears up, their eyes on the cloud of dust bringing Sarah. The wagon passed the fenced field, and the cows and sheep looked up, too. It rounded the windmill and the barn and the windbreak of Russian olive that Mama had planted long ago. Nick began to bark, then Lottie, and the wagon clattered into the yard and stopped by the steps.

"Hush," said Papa to the dogs.

And it was quiet.

Sarah stepped down from the wagon, a cloth bag in her hand. She reached up and took off her yellow bonnet, smoothing back her brown hair into a bun. She was plain and tall.

"Did you bring some sea?" cried Caleb beside me.

"Something from the sea," said Sarah, smiling. "And me." She turned and lifted a black case from the wagon. "And Seal, too."

Carefully she opened the case, and Seal, gray with white feet, stepped out. Lottie lay down, her head on her paws, staring. Nick leaned down to sniff. Then he lay down, too.

"The cat will be good in the barn," said Papa. "For mice."

Sarah smiled. "She will be good in the house, too."

Sarah took Caleb's hand, then mine. Her hands were large and rough. She gave Caleb a shell — a moon snail, she called it — that was curled and smelled of salt.

"The gulls fly high and drop the shells on the rocks below," she told Caleb. "When the shell is broken, they eat what is inside."

"That is very smart," said Caleb.

"For you, Anna," said Sarah, "a sea stone."

And she gave me the smoothest and whitest stone I had ever seen.

"The sea washes over and over and

around the stone, rolling it until it is round and perfect."

"That is very smart, too," said Caleb. He looked up at Sarah. "We do not have the sea here."

Sarah turned and looked out over the plains.

"No," she said. "There is no sea here. But the land rolls a little like the sea."

My father did not see her look, but I did. And I knew that Caleb had seen it, too. Sarah was not smiling. Sarah was already lonely. In a month's time the preacher might come to marry Sarah and Papa. And a month was a long time. Time enough for her to change her mind and leave us.

Papa took Sarah's bags inside, where her room was ready with a quilt on the bed and blue flax dried in a vase on the night table.

Seal stretched and made a small cat sound. I watched her circle the dogs and sniff the air. Caleb came out and stood beside me.

"When will we sing?" he whispered.

I shook my head, turning the white

stone over and over in my hand. I wished everything was as perfect as the stone. I wished that Papa and Caleb and I were perfect for Sarah. I wished we had a sea of our own.

A Home Run for Beth Ann
by Patricia C. McKissack

8

Beth Ann loves baseball, so much that some of the other girls call her a tomboy. What will she do when she has to bake cookies for the Sunday school sweets table? Can tomboys hit home runs and bake? Newbery Honor and Coretta Scott King Award–winner Patricia C. McKissack gives readers a special lesson.

Beth Ann saw the ball coming. She was fast, fast enough to beat it — if she slid. Forgetting it was Sunday, forgetting she had on a pink organdy dress, forgetting everything, Beth Ann lunged for home plate. "Safe," she shouted.

But the catcher disagreed. "Out!" he yelled.

"Safe!" Beth Ann yelled back.

The argument ended abruptly when they spied Miss Emelda Spence coming

43

across the street, stepping fast and with purpose. They all stood stone-still, especially when they saw The Look in Miss Spence's eyes. The Look could make a cobra back down.

"Oh, no," sighed Beth Ann. "I'm in trouble!" It was so unfair, she thought, having Miss Spence as her third-grade teacher all year and then having her as a Sunday school teacher, too. But it seemed Miss Spence had taught everybody, including the twelve apostles.

"Is that *you* we see, Beth Ann Logan?" asked Miss Spence. That's the way Miss Spence talked. She asked questions with answers she already knew, and used "we" in places where most people used "I."

Beth Ann scrambled to her feet, dusted off her legs, and smoothed out the pink organdy dress as best she could. Miss Spence clicked her teeth and shook her head. "This is *not* John and Mae Etta's daughter," she said, "out here in her Sunday best, hollering and screaming, running like a March hare?" Then she strutted away, adding, "Shame on you!"

Beth Ann quickly picked up the lace socks and patent leather shoes she had taken off and followed Miss Spence over to Brown Memorial A.M.E. Church for Sunday school. When she was sure Miss Spence wasn't looking, Beth Ann glanced over her shoulder. She flashed a wide smile at her teammates and made an umpire's signal for safe.

"No," said Miss Spence, never turning around. "You were out!"

Class had already started by the time Beth Ann had washed her face and hands and put on her socks and shoes. "There is a time for everything under the sun," Miss Spence was saying when Beth Ann slipped into her seat, trying hard not to call attention to herself.

Miss Spence raised an eyebrow, then continued. "There is a time to fast and a time to feast. Next Sunday will be a time for feasting. The bishop is coming to worship with us. There's going to be a basket supper after service. This Sunday school class has been asked to set up a sweets table. We expect each of *you* to prepare something tasty from scratch — nothing store-bought. I explained it all here," Miss Spence said, passing out take-home letters and recipes written on note cards. Miss Spence thought for a while. Then she gave Beth Ann the recipe for peanut butter cookies.

The idea of cooking wasn't something that interested Beth Ann. Since baseball had come into her life, she had been hardly able to think of anything else. On her eighth birthday during the summer, she had gone to see the Kansas City Monarchs play against the Birmingham Black Barons. For months now, all she'd been able to think about was hitting, scoring runs, and pitching — pitching hard and fast just like the great Satchel Paige. Just then, all she wanted to do was get back in the game as soon as Sunday school was over.

"I'm a boy. Do I have to fix brownies?" Jesse said.

"Do we hear somebody whining?" asked Miss Spence, handing Jesse a letter. The question was his answer. That's the way Miss Spence talked.

"What about a tomboy?" Agnes Mitchell whispered to Mary Jean Perry loud enough for Beth Ann to hear. They pointed at the large grass stain on her organdy dress, then giggled.

Miss Spence flashed her no-nonsense look. "Did you have something of importance to say?" Miss Spence asked Agnes and Mary Jean.

"No, ma'am," they answered like twin parrots. They were quiet for the rest of Sunday school. But at school the next day, the two girls had plenty to say. They caught up with Beth Ann walking home from school.

"Hey," Agnes called. "What are you supposed to make for the sweets table? I've got to fix ambrosia."

"I'm making gelatin with fruit in it," Mary Jean added.

"I think I'm supposed to bring peanut butter cookies," Beth Ann answered, not really caring.

"You don't know what you're making?" asked Agnes, carrying on like it was so awful. Then she turned up her nose like she smelled something rotten. "What more can you expect from a tomboy?"

"Aggh," Mary Jean said, faking a gag. "I pity the poor soul who eats any of *your* cooking."

And before Beth Ann could say anything back, they crossed the street and hurried away. Usually she didn't care what Agnes and Mary Jean had to say. Most of the time she felt sorry for them. They had never had the joy of hitting a home run over the head of Billy Baker out in center field, and she had. But this wasn't about baseball. Suddenly the idea of cooking became very, very scary.

Beth Ann worried and worried all week. Her pitching was off and her batting average took a nosedive. Thursday night she dreamt that the bishop took one bite of her cookies, turned purple, and fell over dead.

She was frantic by the time she finally made them on Saturday night. Her mother helped read the directions on the recipe. But Beth Ann did all the measuring, mixing, and stirring. When they were out of the oven and cooled, her father tasted one. He said it was good.

A father would say that, no matter what, Beth Ann thought. "They probably taste terrible."

Reluctantly Beth Ann set out for church the next morning, carrying the peanut butter cookies in a basket. All through the service, she wished to be somewhere else, someplace far, far away. As soon as the last hymn was sung and the final amen was said, everybody hurried to the churchyard where the basket supper was served.

"Come, children," said Miss Spence, "it's time to spread our sweets table."

Agnes put out her ambrosia in a pretty glass bowl. Mary Jean arranged fruit gelatin cups in a circle with matching plastic spoons. Even Jesse was proud of the brownies he had made. Miss Spence complimented them all for doing such a fine job. Beth Ann tried to slip away. But it was too late.

"Is that Beth Ann we see, slipping away like a thief in the night?" said Miss

Spence. "Where is your contribution to the sweets table?"

All eyes turned toward Beth Ann. She stood there clutching the basket to her chest. Thinking about the flat, ugly cookies in the basket made her stomach churn. They were all different shapes, some big, some tiny. Some even a little burned.

"Come on, Beth Ann," said Agnes, giving Mary Jean a wink. "Open up the basket and show us what you made."

Beth Ann swallowed hard. She reached in the basket and took out the platter and put it on the table. "I hope there's an ambulance close," said Agnes, choking back a laugh.

Mary Jean didn't try to hold back. She laughed outright. Now everybody was laughing, but they stopped when they saw The Look on Miss Spence's face.

Suddenly, the bishop approached the Sunday school sweets table. "Hello, Miss Spence," he said, speaking warmly. Miss Spence greeted the bishop with a respectful nod and a crisp good afternoon.

The bishop looked at the table. "Your children have done it again," he said. "Everything looks great."

They all beamed with pride — all except Beth Ann.

"Who made the peanut butter cookies?" the bishop asked.

"She did," said Agnes, pointing to Beth Ann.

"Good," he said. "I look forward to getting my fill of peanut butter cookies whenever I come here."

Beth Ann remembered her dream and held her breath as the bishop took a bite. "Ummm!" he said, smacking his lips. To her surprise, he didn't turn purple and he didn't fall over dead. "Wonderful!" he said. "Delicious!"

"Really?" Beth Ann was shocked.

"Really?" said Agnes and Mary Jean. They were put out. They looked like two carnival dolls dangling on a string, one dressed in yellow and the other in blue. They didn't know what to say.

For a split second Beth Ann thought she saw Miss Emelda Spence smile. "What did we learn from this?" she asked

Beth Ann later as they served dessert to others who came through the line.

Beth Ann thought for a moment. "Well," she began, "I learned a lot. But most of all I found out that there's more than one way to hit a home run."

The Rare Spotted Birthday Party
by Margaret Mahy

8

Mark still wants to have a birthday party even though he has the measles. But you can't have a measle party, can you?

It was Mark's birthday in two days, but he was not happy about it.

His mother had made a wonderful cake, round, brown, and full of nuts and raisins and cherries. There were balloons and party hats hidden in the high cupboard with the Christmas decorations and old picture books. But Mark was not happy.

It was his birthday in two days and he had the measles.

Everyone was getting the measles.

"Measles are going around," said Mark's little sister Sarah.

John with the sticking-out ears had the measles.

The twins next door — James and Gerald — had the measles. They had the same brown hair, the same brown eyes, and now they both had the same brown spots.

Mark's friend, Mousey, had the measles. Mousey had so many freckles everyone was surprised that measles could find any room on him.

"Mousey must be even more spotted than I am," said Mark.

"Mousey must be more spotted than *anyone*," Sarah said. "He is a rare spotted mouse."

"It's worse for me," said Mark. "No one can have a birthday when they are covered in spots."

"No one would be able to come," said Sarah, "Do you feel sick, Mark?"

"I feel a bit sick," said Mark. "Even if I *could* have a birthday, I don't think I would want it."

"That is the worst thing," said Sarah. "Not even *wanting* a birthday is worst of all."

Two days later, when the birthday

really came, Mark did not feel sick any more. He just felt spotty.

He opened his presents at breakfast.

His mother and father had given him a camera. It was small, but it would take real pictures. Sarah gave him a paint box. (She always gave him a paint box. Whenever Mark got a new paint box, he gave Sarah the old one.)

All morning they painted.

"It feels funny today," said Mark. "It doesn't feel like a birthday. It doesn't feel special at all."

Sarah had painted a class of children. Now she began to paint spots on them.

Lunch was plain and healthy.

In the afternoon Mark's mother started to brush him all over. She brushed his hair. She brushed his bathrobe, though it was new and did not need brushing. She brushed his slippers.

"We will have a birthday drive," she said. "The car windows will stop the measles from getting out."

They drove out into the country and up a hill that Mark knew. "There's Peter's house," he said. "Peter-up-the-hill! He has measles, too."

"We might pay him a visit for a moment," Mark's mother said. "He won't catch measles from you if he has them already."

The front door was open. They rang the bell and walked in. Then Mark got a real surprise! The room was full of people. Lots of the people were boys wearing bathrobes — all of them spotty boys, MEASLE-Y boys.

"Happy birthday! Happy birthday!" they shouted.

There was John with the sticking-out ears. His ears were still a bit spotty around the edges. There were the twins, James and Gerald. Measles made them look more like each other than ever before. There was Mousey. You could not tell where his freckles left off and his measles began. There was Peter-up-the-hill in a red bathrobe, and Peter-next-to-the-shop in a bluey-green one.

"Happy birthday! Happy birthday!" they all shouted.

"It's a measle party," Mark's mother explained. "So many people are getting over measles we decided to have a measle party on your birthday."

"Have you brought my birthday cake?" asked Mark.

"It is in a box in the back of the car," said his mother. "I would not forget an important thing like that."

What a funny, spotty, measle-y party! All the guests except Sarah were wearing bathrobes.

They played a game called "Painting Spots on an Elephant." They played "Measle-y Chairs" (this is like "Musical Chairs" except that people who play it have to have the measles).

Sarah found a piece of blue chalk and drew spots all over her face. "I've got *blue* measles," she said. "Mine are very unusual spots." (She did not like being the only person without any spots at all.)

Then came the party food. They had spaghetti and meatballs. They had fruit salad and ice cream, and glasses of orange juice. The fruit salad had strawberries and grapes in it.

Then Mark's mother brought in the

cake she had made. It was frosted with white icing, and it was spotted and dotted and spattered with pink dots.

"Measles!" cried Mark. "The cake's got measles!" He thought it was the funniest, nicest cake he had ever seen. The measles made it taste extremely delicious.

A measle cake for a measle party! A spotty cake for a dotty party!

"I don't think I'll have a piece of cake," said Sarah. "I don't feel very well. . . . I feel all hot and cross."

"Heigh-ho!" said Mark's mother. "I think I know what is wrong."

"You are probably getting the measles," said Mark. "Perhaps *you* will have a measle party, too."

"We will think of something else for Sarah," said his mother. "But now we must go home."

"Can't I have a measle party as well?" Sarah pleaded. "I want one, too."

"Measle parties are like comets," said Mark's mother. "If you see one in twenty years you are lucky."

She took Mark and Sarah home, with

Mark thinking to himself that it was worth getting the measles at birthday time if a special measles party was the result.

After all, not many people have been to one.

8 x 2 = Sweet Sixteen
by Ann M. Martin

Many readers know Karen Brewster as the star of the Baby-sitters Little Sister, Ann M. Martin's best-selling series. When Karen is planning to have two parties for her eighth birthday, she decides that she's not really turning eight, but sweet sixteen. Surely sixteen is better than plain old eight. . . .

My name is Karen Brewer. I have freckles and I wear glasses. I live in Stoneybrook, Connecticut. I am seven years old. But not for long. Very soon I will turn eight. I have been waiting for this for a long time. I have been waiting since I turned seven.

My birthday will be in three weeks. I am going to have *two* parties. This is because my little brother, Andrew, and I live in two houses. Every other month we live with our mother and stepfather, Seth, in one house. In between, we live with our father, stepmother, stepsister, stepbrothers, adopted sister, and stepgrandmother across town in another house. Sometimes having two homes and two families is confusing. Mostly, I like it very much.

Guess what. Yesterday I told Andrew that since I am going to have two parties that means I will turn eight twice. This makes me sixteen. Sixteen is a very wonderful age. I asked my mother if I could have a sweet sixteen party, and she said no, not until I am actually sixteen. I pointed out that when I am sixteen and have two sweet sixteen parties I will turn thirty-two, and Mommy said, "Just think. When you are seventy-nine, you will turn one hundred and fifty-eight. Won't that be something?" Mommy does not always take me seriously. I knew then that she would not let me have a sweet sixteen party. Not yet. So I just planned two regular eight-year-old parties. But I could not stop thinking about being sixteen years old.

"Karen," said Mommy one morning, "have you made your birthday list yet? I would like to get your presents. Your father would probably like a list too."

Well, for heaven's sake. Do you know what? I had not even thought about my birthday lists. I had been too busy thinking about turning sixteen.

"I have *not* made them yet!" I cried. "I forgot. But I will make them right now."

I ran upstairs to my room. I sat down at my desk. I found a pad of paper and my pen that writes in three colors. I chose pink. I decided to make the list for Mommy first.

I made a list of things I was *pretty* sure Mommy could get for me — a scrapbook, a sweatshirt, a glitter-art kit. It is always better to make a list like that. One year I asked for a go-cart, a playhouse, a kitten, and my own TV. That was silly. Mommy could not get me those things, so then she just had to guess what I wanted.

I put Mommy's list aside and started Daddy's. The last two things on Daddy's list were:

swing set for the backyard? (we could all enjoy it)
bedtime 1/2 hour later

I looked at my two lists. I thought about them for awhile. Then I started a third list. I just could not stop thinking about turning sixteen. On top of that third piece of paper I wrote:

WHAT I WANT FOR MY 16TH BIRTHDAY

I stared out the window and thought for awhile. Bedtime one-half hour later was fine, but what I really wanted was to stay up all night. If I were sixteen I could do that. I wrote:

1. NO bedtime AT ALL

I *know* that things go on at night after I have gone to bed, and I would like to find out what they are. What do the grown-ups do at night? I think they talk to their friends on the phone and watch good stuff on TV. But I will never know unless I can stay up after 8:30.

I thought some more. Then I wrote:

2. I would like to drive a car, or at least be allowed to use the lawn mower.

I am not sure, but I *think* that sixteen-year-olds can drive. At least, here in Stoneybrook they can drive. And that is one thing I really, really want to do. If I could drive I could go wherever I wanted whenever I wanted. I would not have to wait for someone to say, "Karen, I am going to the hardware store. Do you want to come with me?" The hardware store is *so* boring, but sometimes I go along just *in case* we might be able to go to the toy store afterward. Then there is the lawn mower. Daddy's is like a little car. If I could not drive a real car, at least I could drive the lawn mower.

I continued my list.

3. I want to go to a big fancy party (NOT a birthday party) and wear a long sparkly gown.

Last year when my big stepbrother Charlie was sixteen he went to a dance at his high school. It was called a junior prom. But it was not just any dance. It was also a party. And the people (most of them were sixteen like Charlie) who went to it got *very* dressed up. Charlie wore a tuxedo. Even better, the girl he took to the dance wore a long gown. It was pink and covered with sequins. It was the most beautiful gown I have ever seen. The girl's name was Joanna, and she and Charlie got to stay out until after midnight. I want to do that. I want to wear a gown like

Joanna's and go to a prom and stay out until after midnight. And then I want to drive myself home.

4. I want to take a trip all by myself.

Now, I do *not* mean getting on a plane without my parents and letting a flight attendant take charge of me while I fly to my grandmother's farm. I have done that before and it is not like taking a trip by myself. What I mean is that I would decide to go to Italy and then I would drive myself to the airport and get on a plane, with*out* help from a flight attendant, and fly to the city of Rome. In Rome I would stay in a hotel and go sightseeing and stay out as late as I want. Also, I would go to fancy restaurants and order pizza for every meal.

5. I would like to have a real job, like an after-school job, and earn a real paycheck.

A real job is so grown-up. I cannot wait for my first job. I would like to work in an office. I would get to use a fancy computer, and send people information on a fax machine. If I could be in charge of some people that would be even better. I am pretty good at ordering people around and making decisions. I think I would also be good in a meeting. I do not know if sixteen-year-olds can get jobs like this, though. Charlie is *seventeen*, and his after-school job is at a grocery store. I think he puts people's groceries into bags. Oh, well. Just so I get a paycheck. Because as soon as I start earning some money I will save for a car and that trip to Rome.

6. I want to go to a football game with my grown-up high-school friends.

When you are eight and you want to go somewhere with your friends, somebody's parent has to drive you. Or maybe a baby-sitter goes with you. But I want to pick up my best friends in my own car and drive us to the high school for . . . a football game. Charlie is *always* driving his friends to football games. I know they have a good time. They sit together up high in the bleachers and eat hot dogs and potato chips. And when their team makes a touchdown they jump up and down and sometimes they cheer. High-school cheers are very cool. Not like "two-four-six-eight, who do you appreciate?" That is for babies. High-school cheers are about win-ning and fighting, and some of them sound like rap songs. My friends and I would shout and hug each other after each touchdown. And then I would say, "Does anybody want another hot dog? My treat. I just got my paycheck."

    7. Go to Magic Adventure Amusement Park and take the Fear Mountain ride.

Here is the thing. I am not yet tall enough to take the Fear Mountain ride. Mommy and Seth and Andrew and I went to Magic Adventure two months ago and I had been waiting and waiting for Fear Mountain. But when we got to the line for Fear Mountain we saw a notice that said in order to go on the ride you must be as tall as the top of the sign. And I was not tall enough. (Neither was Andrew.) I was mad. I even talked to the person in charge of the ride, but she said, "Sorry, no excep-tions." Well. If I were sixteen I would be tall enough. I think Magic Adventure is the very first place I would go in my new car with my paycheck.

8. I want to be allowed to wear glitter makeup on my lips and eyes. In public.

This is the last thing I would want for my sixteenth birthday. I have seen girls wearing this makeup. (Actually, I have seen a few boys wearing it, too.) It is *very* cool. It comes in lots of different colors. I know where you can get it. At Cosmetics 'N' More. It comes in little pots that look like paint jars, and you just dab it on with your finger. You can put it on your lips like lipstick, on your eyelids, even on your cheeks. You can make your whole face glittery. Once I asked Mommy if I could wear glitter makeup, and she said, "Well, okay, but not in public." I knew what that meant. It meant I could wear it for dress-up. But I want to wear it for real — when I'm out late driving around Italy in my own car that I have bought with paychecks from my job.

When I had finished my list, I read it several times. I wondered if I really could do all those things when I turn sixteen.

Maybe, maybe not. I looked at the lists I had made for Mommy and Daddy. And then I made one tiny little change on Daddy's list. I erased "1/2." In its place I wrote "one." "Bedtime one hour later." There. That was something. It was a little closer to being sixteen and having no bedtime at all.

Then I had a thought. I am eight years old now (almost). It will take me another eight years to reach sixteen. My first eight years have seemed a very long time, but they have been a lot of fun. Maybe I should not wish the next eight years away. I should probably enjoy them. I can have fun dreaming about being sixteen.

I picked up the list for Mommy. I carried it downstairs. And I imagined myself walking down the stairs in my sparkly pink gown, ready for the junior prom — in eight years, when I really am sweet sixteen.

From
One of the Third Grade Thonkers
by Phyllis Reynolds Naylor

8

Jimmy plans on spending his spring vacation with his club, the Thonkers. That is, until he finds out his weirdo cousin David is coming to stay with them. Jimmy is the number-one Thonker. But they're the third grade Thonkers, and wimpy David is only in second grade. What are the rest of the Thonkers going to think of Jimmy now?

Three things happened to Jimmy Novak when he was in the third grade.

His mother had a baby, which wasn't bad, because every time people brought Benjamin a present, they brought a little something for Jimmy as well.

Next, Jimmy hurt his knee and had an operation, which wasn't the best thing in the world to have happen, but it wasn't the worst, either.

And finally, a cousin came to visit who

was the last person in the world Jimmy wanted to see. But that didn't happen until later.

It was after the operation that Jimmy first heard the word *Thonker*. Dr. Sheen, the surgeon, was a little bit nuts.

"Hi, Thonker, how you doing this morning?" he said each time he came into Jimmy's room. And after Jimmy left the hospital and went to Dr. Sheen's office for visits, the doctor would say, "Just climb up on the table, Thonker, and let me look at that knee."

On one of Jimmy's visits to the doctor, he saw his friend from school, Sam Angelino, and realized that Dr. Sheen called all his patients "Thonkers," which showed just how crazy he really was.

"See you in three weeks, Thonker," he said as Jimmy started out the door, and then, to Sam, who had broken his arm on the slide, "Come on in here, Thonker, and let's see how you're doing."

Jimmy and Sam grinned at each other. The next day at school they called themselves "Dr. Bonkers' Thonkers," and the name stuck.

It wasn't a club at first. It was only Jimmy and Sam walking around the playground, with the other boys tagging behind. Jimmy was on crutches and Sam had his arm in a cast, and every day at recess, the other boys begged to try out the crutches or to write their names on Sam's cast. They wanted to know what an operation was like and whether Jimmy had felt any pain when he was asleep. Jimmy said maybe he did feel a little something when the doctor started cutting, even though the last thing he remembered was his dad giving him the thumbs-up sign in the hallway.

The other boys talked, too, about how Sam had fallen backward down the steps of the slide and hadn't cried, even though they could see the bump on his arm where the bone had broken. It was understood that if you were going to be a Thonker, you ought to be a little braver than the other children; something had to have happened that you wouldn't want to go through again in a million years.

So when Peter Nilsson came to school one morning with the story of how the brakes had failed on his mother's car at the drawbridge — the car with him and his mother in it — and how the car had almost, but not quite, gone in the canal, Peter became one of the Thonkers, too. Even the teacher had heard about the accident on the evening news.

From then on it was just the three of them — Jimmy, Sam, and Peter — but there wasn't another boy in the whole third grade who didn't wish that he, too, was a Thonker.

They had special T-shirts, for one thing. In Jimmy's, Sam's, and Peter's families, however, you didn't just walk up to your mom and say, "I want a T-shirt with *Thonker* on the front." You said, "What can I do to earn some money for a T-shirt?" Jimmy had to hose out the garbage cans and paint them; Peter had to scrub the front porch and wash some windows; and Sam had to baby-sit his little sister and change her diaper twice. But the next day, all three boys came to school in new black T-shirts with the word *Thonker* on the front, in big red letters dripping blood, and on the back of each T-shirt it said, *Do or Die*.

They always rode their bikes in formation, too. Sam decided that they ought to rank themselves according to how long each of them had had to be brave. Jimmy, it was decided, was Number One, because it took a lot longer to get well after a knee operation than it did after a broken arm. They argued about who would be Number Two, because almost going off the end of the bridge into the canal was scary as anything for Peter, but since the fear only lasted a minute, it was decided that Sam with his broken arm would be Thonker Number Two. So whenever they rode around Garnsey Park or over to Holy Cross School, Jimmy, who was the largest, went first; Sam, who was shortest and heaviest, came next; and Peter, who was tall, brought up the rear.

By the time March came around, Jimmy decided that third grade wasn't so bad. He had a new baby brother, lots of new gifts, and he himself was Thonker Number One.

And then, the third thing happened: The cousin came.

The week had started out well, actually. The wind felt warmer, and the Thonkers were already talking about what they were going to do over spring vacation. The Novaks' house was on a street at the very top of a steep hill. The hill was so steep that the Novaks' backyard sloped all the way down to the alley. The garage, in fact, was built under the end of the backyard, like a cave.

Jimmy's dad said he was tired of driving his car all the way around to the alley, and that, if Jimmy liked, the Thonkers could use the garage for a clubhouse — till next winter, anyway. Jimmy was in heaven.

It was *then* that the third thing happened, the worst thing, the cousin from Cincinnati. Mother got a call from her sister, Lois, who was going to have a heart operation. Lois wanted to send seven-year-old David to stay with the Novaks until she recovered. He would be flying up the week before spring vacation.

Jimmy walked slowly out the door and

down the backyard. He climbed over the fence at the bottom, dropped to the alley, and opened the door to the clubhouse.

It was cool inside the garage, with only the light from the door coming in. Jimmy sat down heavily in one of the chairs and stared at the words Sam had painted on the wall: "The Thonkers, Rough, Tough, and Terrible."

A year ago, when Jimmy had last seen his cousin, David cried when he hurt his mouth eating a Frito; he got scared in a movie and Aunt Lois had to take him home; he carried around a large teddy bear with one leg missing; and he still wet the bed. And now, that very same cousin was coming here.

On Monday, Sam Angelino and Peter Nilsson stopped by for Jimmy on their way to school. The Third Grade Thonkers always walked together. Jimmy went outside where Sam was waiting in his brown leather jacket. Peter Nilsson was wearing a sweat shirt with a picture of a giant fist on the back. Jimmy himself was wearing his football jersey with the padded shoulders. Then David came out wearing a wool sweater with red and green reindeer on it and carrying his "Little House on the Prairie" lunch bucket.

"Who's *that*?" Sam whispered.

"This is my cousin, David. He's staying with us for a while," Jimmy told them.

"Hi," said David, and as the three Thonkers started off, he tagged along behind.

Jimmy had promised his mother that he would show David to the second grade classroom, where he would be going to school until Aunt Lois was better.

"This is David," Jimmy said to the second grade teacher. All the other children in the room were staring.

"We're glad to have you, David," said the teacher. "Jimmy's mother told me you'd be staying with us a while. Just put your lunch bucket back there with the others, and we'll find a place for you to sit."

"See you," said Jimmy, and went on down the hall.

"How long is he going to be here?" Peter asked Jimmy as they took their seats in Miss Verona's classroom.

"Till his mother's better; she's having an operation," Jimmy said.

"I can't believe he's *your* cousin!" Sam told him. "He looks like he belongs in nursery school."

"He's not going to be hanging around with *us,* is he?" Peter asked. "He's not going to be one of the Thonkers?"

"No way," said Jimmy.

All morning long Jimmy hoped that David would make new friends in second grade and have someone else to talk to. But when noon came and the first, second, and third graders gathered in the all-purpose room for lunch, David brought his "Little House on the Prairie" lunch bucket right over to the table where the Thonkers were sitting, opened it up, and made a face at everything Jimmy's mother had packed for him.

"I don't like salami, I don't like oranges, and I don't like oatmeal cookies," he whined. "Doesn't anyone have a Twinkie?"

"Eat it," said Jimmy, frowning.

"I'll trade mine for yours," David said to Sam. "What kind of sandwich do you have?"

"Chicken gizzards," said Sam, hiding a smile.

David stared. He turned to Peter. "What's yours?"

Peter pretended to peek between his two slices of bread. "Liver and horseradish," he said.

David's mouth twitched. He glumly pulled all the crusts off his salami sandwich and took a tiny bite.

When afternoon recess came around, Jimmy and Sam and Peter started a game of kickball in one corner of the field. David tried to join in, but the first time the ball hit his leg, David limped over to the fence, rubbing his shin.

Well, he'll just have to find some friends his own age to play with, Jimmy thought later as he copied his spelling words from the blackboard. Letting David sleep in his room and walk to school beside him every day was enough. Jimmy certainly didn't have to play with him all the time.

During the last hour of the day, as the

students were turning in their history papers, Jimmy stapled them together for Miss Verona and got a staple in his thumb by accident.

"Ouch!" he said softly.

"Wow!" said Peter, staring at the staple stuck partway in Jimmy's thumb. "Bionic man! Let me try that!"

He took the stapler, gave it a press, and the staple must have gone in a little deeper because Peter sucked in his breath. But when Sam tried it, he didn't make any noise at all, and there they were — the three Thonkers with staples stuck halfway into their thumbs.

When the bell rang, they went outside to wait for David, trying not to laugh.

Peter took a stick of gum from his jeans. "Want some gum?" he asked Jimmy's cousin.

"I only eat Juicy Fruit," said David.

"You're in luck," said Peter, holding it out. As David took it, his eyes fell on the staple. He gave a little scream and backed away.

"What's that stuck in your thumb?" he squealed. "Pull it out!"

Peter pretended to notice it for the first time. "Oh, yeah," he said. "I guess it's a staple."

"Well, what do you know?" said Sam. "I've got one, too!"

"So do I!" said Jimmy.

"H-how did they get there?" David asked.

"Well, we're a club, see," Sam told him. "The Thonkers. You hang around with us, you've got to get staples in your thumbs and everything."

With that, the three Thonkers sauntered on home, David trailing behind, holding his "Little House on the Prairie" lunch bucket in one hand, his Flintstones pencil box in the other, wearing his bright wool sweater with the red and green reindeer on the front, and looking worried.

From
Someday Angeline
by Louis Sachar

8

If your first word is "octopus," you know you're going to be a little different. No one thinks it's so great that Angeline is so smart, especially Angeline. Sometimes people even call her a freak. Ever since her mom died, it's been even harder. How would you like to be in sixth grade and still suck your thumb?

Angeline was put in the sixth grade. They put her there because, well, they had to put her somewhere and they didn't know where else to put her. They put her in Mrs. Hardlick's class and that was probably the worst place to be put. She sat at the back of the room.

She started to put her thumb in her mouth but caught herself. She was smart enough for the sixth grade. She was the smartest person in the class, but she still did dumb things like suck her thumb. She knew Mrs. Hardlick hated it when she sucked her thumb. Sixth-graders are not supposed to suck their thumbs. She also cried too much for the sixth grade.

"Who was Christopher Columbus?" Mrs. Hardlick asked the class.

Angeline was the only one who raised her hand.

Mrs. Hardlick looked annoyed. "Somebody else this time," she said and glared at Angeline. "It's always the same people."

Angeline lowered her hand. It wasn't her fault she was the only one. She didn't think Mrs. Hardlick should have been mad at *her* for raising *her* hand. It was everybody else's fault for not raising theirs. But in her mind she could hear Mrs. Hardlick saying sarcastically, "It's always everybody else's fault, never your own." As she thought this, her thumb slipped into her mouth.

Mrs. Hardlick told the class about Columbus. She said that Columbus discovered America.

Angeline knew that was wrong. How

could Columbus have discovered America when there were already lots of people here when he arrived? She knew that America was actually first discovered by the first snail to crawl out of water and onto land. It was something she knew before she was born.

However, she tried to give both Mrs. Hardlick and Mr. Columbus the benefit of the doubt. "Maybe," she thought, *"from his own point of view* Columbus discovered America." But that didn't seem true either because even after Columbus got here, he still didn't know he was in America. He thought he was in India, which was why he called Americans "Indians."

Mrs. Hardlick said that Columbus proved the world was round.

Angeline knew that was also wrong. If he really had made it to India, *then* he would have proved it was round because India was east and he sailed west. But he bumped into America first and he could have sailed to America even if the world was flat.

Besides, everybody knows the world is

round before they are born. That's why nobody is even slightly surprised when they first learn it in school.

These were the thoughts occupying Angeline's mind when Mrs. Hardlick suddenly called her name. "Angeline!" she commanded. "Take your thumb out of your mouth right now!"

"Oops," she thought as she quickly pulled it out.

"We don't suck our thumbs in the sixth grade," said Mrs. Hardlick proudly.

She heard some of the other sixth-graders snicker.

Mrs. Hardlick resented Angeline. She didn't like having an eight-year-old kid in her class of sixth-graders. She especially didn't like having an eight-year-old kid who was smarter than she, although Mrs. Hardlick would never admit that Angeline was smart. In Mrs. Hardlick's mind, Angeline was a genius, which had nothing to do with being smart. It was more like being a freak, like a goat with two heads.

"Only babies suck their thumbs," said Mrs. Hardlick.

Angeline felt ashamed. Even kids in the

third grade, her age, didn't suck their thumbs anymore. She felt like she was going to cry. "Oh, come on, Angeline," she told herself. "Don't start crying. Not now!" She cried way too much for the sixth grade. She even cried a lot for the first grade.

"Look, she's crying," someone teased.

She was not. It wasn't true. But then, as soon as she heard that person say it, then, wouldn't you know it, she did start to cry.

"She may be smart but she's still a baby," said someone else.

"She's not smart, she's a freak."

"Angeline, don't be a crybaby," Mrs. Hardlick admonished her. "If you feel you must cry, go outside. You may come back in when you are ready to act like a sixth-grader."

Still crying, Angeline walked outside.

"What a freak," she heard someone say.

She sat down outside, next to the door. She was wrong. Mrs. Hardlick didn't hate it when she sucked her thumb. It was just the opposite. Mrs. Hardlick loved it. The whole class loved it. They loved to put her down. And whether she realized it or not, that was why she cried. It wasn't because they called her a baby or a freak; it was because they enjoyed it so much.

She bit the tip of her thumb and sniffled. She felt just like a double-headed goat.

From
Go Fish
by Mary Stolz

8

After a day of fishing, Thomas settles onto the porch with his grandfather and their cat, Ringo, to hear faraway stories about faraway places. Even when you're eight, you're not too old for a magical bedtime story.

After the card game, they consulted the TV section of the newspaper. Finding nothing that Grandfather said they wanted to see, they went out to the porch and sat on the swing, creaking idly back and forth. Ringo, abandoning the lizard, followed and resumed his railing perch.

The sun flew citrus-colored banners as it sank into the Gulf of Mexico. Cradle songs fell from leafy branches, and crickets scraped their fiddles in the grass. On the ground a pair of mockingbirds hopped around each other, flicking their tails, then lost interest and flew apart.

Ringo watched, but made no move toward them.

Thomas yawned. "You could tell me a story," he said.

"All right. What about?"

"You pick. Only not a bad one."

"Do I ever tell you a bad story?"

"I guess I mean not a sad one."

"I see. Only happy people with happy problems, as the old saying goes?"

"Grandfather! That sounds silly."

"It is silly. I try to tell you about life, and life is not full of happy people with happy problems."

Thomas turned and looked into his grandfather's eyes. "I know that already," he said. "I've known that for a long time."

Grandfather put his arm around Thomas and held him close. "Of course," he said, with a whistly sigh. "We know that, don't we?"

Thomas leaned his head against the thin chest. "Did your grandfather tell you stories?" he asked.

"He did."

"And did his grandfather tell him stories?"

"Yes."

"And did —"

"You could keep that up till we were
face to face with your great-great-great-
and-one-more-great-grandfather. He who
was taken a slave from his home in Benin."

"In Africa."

"Yes. Would you like to hear an African
story?"

"Yes. But make it up, please."

According to Grandfather, *his* great-
grandfather had said all the family on that
side was descended from the Yorubas,
from that great-great-great-and-one-more-
great-grandfather and his long-ago wife.
Grandfather had a store of African tales,
mostly Yoruban, passed down the genera-
tions since then. He told true stories,
which were history. And folktales, which
were mythology. *And* he had a gift for
making up stories. Thomas usually liked
those best.

It seemed to him that perfect truth, like
perfect honesty, came out sometimes to
perfect misery.

"Make one up," he said again, and yawned.

Grandfather tipped his head back, thought for a few minutes, and began:

"You must understand, Thomas, that certain Yoruba tribes had the cult of *ibeji*."

Thomas sighed happily. African words! *Iguneromwo Ikegobo. Uhumwelao*. He didn't always remember what they meant, but loved the sound of them.

"What's a cult?" he asked.

"A belief."

"I see. What is *ibeji*?"

"*Ibeji* are twins."

"I see. Go on with the story."

"If I'm permitted to. The cult of *ibeji* held that twins were unlucky for the tribe. Therefore such children were always separated, one sent to a village east, the other to a village west of the village where they were born."

"Why?"

"Thomas, I don't *know* why. It's just what my grandfather said his grandfather said his grandfather — and so on back — said was fact. Shall I continue?"

"Oh, yes."

"Fine. Now, let's see." Again Grandfather paused to gather his thoughts. He made up his stories as he went along, which required a certain amount of thinking. Thomas tried to wait patiently.

"All right, here it is, Thomas. Once upon a time, long long ago, in the beginning of the world, Shango, the thunder god, and his wife —"

"What was her name?"

Grandfather exhaled a breath. "Her name was — was Esigie."

"You're making that up."

"I'm making the whole thing up."

"Go on," said Thomas, trying to stifle another yawn.

"Very well, Esigie gave birth to a pair of sons. Twins. Knowing that misfortune would befall the tribe if the twins, the *ibeji*, remained together, Shango transformed them into two winds, sending one to the east and the other to the west of the place where he and Esigie made their home."

Thomas's eyes drooped. His grandfather's voice seemed far away. "What happened then?" he murmured.

"The brothers, the east wind and the west wind, wanted to come together again, and that is why they blow around the world to this day, always trying to find each other but never able to."

"Poor *ibeji*," said Thomas, dropping into sleep.

Grandfather remained, holding his grandson, while the sky darkened and the evening star rose from the sea. A barred owl flew by like a great brown moth, so close that Grandfather could almost count his feathers, could have met his eyes if the owl had turned his way.

When Ringo leaped from the railing and disappeared into the cricket-humming garden, and the kitchen clock, only a minute or so behind the bell of the Congregational church, tolled nine o'clock, he gently awakened Thomas and steered him toward bed.

From
Charlotte's Web
by E. B. White

When Fern saves a piglet named Wilbur from being killed, she discovers a magical world in the barn, and a storyteller named Charlotte. But there's just one thing: Charlotte tells her stories from her web, because she's a spider! All of the animals in the barn talk, but Fern's the only one smart enough to listen.

The next day was Saturday. Fern stood at the kitchen sink drying the breakfast dishes as her mother washed them. Mrs. Arable worked silently. She hoped Fern would go out and play with other children, instead of heading for the Zuckermans' barn to sit and watch animals.

"Charlotte is the best storyteller I ever heard," said Fern, poking her dish towel into a cereal bowl.

"Fern," said her mother sternly, "you

must not invent things. You know spiders don't tell stories. Spiders can't talk."

"Charlotte can," replied Fern. "She doesn't talk very loud, but she talks."

"What kind of story did she tell?" asked Mrs. Arable.

"Well," began Fern, "she told us about a cousin of hers who caught a fish in her web. Don't you think that's fascinating?"

"Fern, dear, how would a fish get in a spider's web?" said Mrs. Arable. "You know it couldn't happen. You're making this up."

"Oh, it happened all right," replied Fern. "Charlotte never fibs. This cousin of hers built a web across a stream. One day she was hanging around on the web and a tiny fish leaped into the air and got tangled in the web. The fish was caught by one fin, Mother; its tail was wildly thrashing and shining in the sun. Can't you just see the web, sagging dangerously under the weight of the fish? Charlotte's cousin kept slipping in, dodging out, and she was beaten mercilessly over the head by the wildly thrashing fish, dancing in, dancing out, throwing . . ."

"Fern!" snapped her mother. "Stop it! Stop inventing these wild tales!"

"I'm not inventing," said Fern. "I'm just telling you the facts."

"What finally happened?" asked her mother, whose curiosity began to get the better of her.

"Charlotte's cousin won. She wrapped the fish up, then she ate him when she got good and ready. Spiders have to eat, the same as the rest of us."

"Yes, I suppose they do," said Mrs. Arable, vaguely.

"Charlotte has another cousin who is a balloonist. She stands on her head, lets out a lot of line, and is carried aloft on the wind. Mother, wouldn't you simply love to do that?"

"Yes, I would, come to think of it," replied Mrs. Arable. "But Fern, darling, I wish you would play outdoors today instead of going to Uncle Homer's barn. Find some of your playmates and do something nice outdoors. You're spending too much time in that barn — it isn't good for you to be alone so much."

"Alone?" said Fern. "Alone? My best

friends are in the barn cellar. It is a very sociable place. Not at all lonely."

Fern disappeared after a while, walking down the road toward Zuckermans'. Her mother dusted the sitting room. As she worked she kept thinking about Fern. It didn't seem natural for a little girl to be so interested in animals. Finally Mrs. Arable made up her mind she would pay a call on old Doctor Dorian and ask his advice. She got in the car and drove to his office in the village.

Dr. Dorian had a thick beard. He was glad to see Mrs. Arable and gave her a comfortable chair.

"It's about Fern," she explained. "Fern spends entirely too much time in the Zuckermans' barn. It doesn't seem normal. She sits on a milk stool in a corner of the barn cellar, near the pigpen, and watches animals, hour after hour. She just sits and listens."

Dr. Dorian leaned back and closed his eyes.

"How enchanting!" he said. "It must be real nice and quiet down there. Homer has some sheep, hasn't he?"

"Yes," said Mrs. Arable. "But it all started with that pig we let Fern raise on a bottle. She calls him Wilbur. Homer bought the pig, and ever since it left our place Fern has been going to her uncle's to be near it."

"I've been hearing things about that pig," said Dr. Dorian, opening his eyes. "They say he's quite a pig."

"Have you heard about the words that appeared in the spider's web?" asked Mrs. Arable nervously.

"Yes," replied the doctor.

"Well, do you understand it?" asked Mrs. Arable.

"Understand what?"

"Do you understand how there could be any writing in a spider's web?"

"Oh, no," said Dr. Dorian. "I don't understand it. But for that matter I don't understand how a spider learned to spin a web in the first place. When the words appeared, everyone said they were a miracle. But nobody pointed out that the web itself is a miracle."

"What's miraculous about a spider's web?" said Mrs. Arable. "I don't see why you say a web is a miracle — it's just a web."

"Ever try to spin one?" asked Dr. Dorian.

Mrs. Arable shifted uneasily in her chair. "No," she replied. "But I can crochet a doily and I can knit a sock."

"Sure," said the doctor. "But somebody taught you, didn't they?"

"My mother taught me."

"Well, who taught a spider? A young spider knows how to spin a web without any instructions from anybody. Don't you regard that as a miracle?"

"I suppose so," said Mrs. Arable. "I never looked at it that way before. Still, I don't understand how those words got into the web. I don't understand it, and I don't like what I can't understand."

"None of us do," said Dr. Dorian, sighing. "I'm a doctor. Doctors are supposed to understand everything. But I don't understand everything, and I don't intend to let it worry me."

Mrs. Arable fidgeted. "Fern says the animals talk to each other. Dr. Dorian, do you believe animals talk?"

"I never heard one say anything," he replied. "But that proves nothing. It is quite possible that an animal has spoken civilly to me and that I didn't catch the remark because I wasn't paying attention. Children pay better attention than grownups. If Fern says that the animals in Zuckerman's barn talk, I'm quite ready to believe her. Perhaps if people talked less, animals would talk more. People are incessant talkers — I can give you my word on that."

"Well, I feel better about Fern," said Mrs. Arable. "You don't think I need worry about her?"

"Does she look well?" asked the doctor.

"Oh, yes."

"Appetite good?"

"Oh, yes, she's always hungry."

"Sleep well at night?"

"Oh, yes."

"Then don't worry," said the doctor.

"Do you think she'll ever start thinking about something besides pigs and sheep and geese and spiders?"

"How old is Fern?"

"She's eight."

"Well," said Dr. Dorian, "I think she will always love animals. But I doubt that she spends her entire life in Homer Zuckerman's barn cellar. How about boys — does she know any boys?"

"She knows Henry Fussy," said Mrs. Arable brightly.

Dr. Dorian closed his eyes again and went into deep thought. "Henry Fussy," he mumbled. "Hmm. Remarkable. Well, I don't think you have anything to worry about. Let Fern associate with her friends in the barn if she wants to. I would say, offhand, that spiders and pigs were fully as interesting as Henry Fussy. Yet I predict that the day will come when even Henry will drop some chance remark that catches Fern's attention. It's amazing how children change from year to year. How's Avery?" he asked, opening his eyes wide.

"Oh, Avery," chuckled Mrs. Arable. "Avery is always fine. Of course, he gets into poison ivy and gets stung by wasps and bees and brings frogs and snakes home and breaks everything he lays his hands on. He's fine."

"Good!" said the doctor.

Mrs. Arable said goodbye and thanked Dr. Dorian very much for his advice. She felt greatly relieved.